Tang's
Happy Day

It was a beautiful sunny day on Zing Zilla Island.

The lovely day meant Tang was feeling really happy.

He decided he wanted to write a song.
"But what sort of song do you sing on a sunny day?" thought Tang.

Just then, Tang heard
some beautiful,
happy music coming
from the Glade.

He decided to go
and investigate.

DJ Loose was waiting for Tang in the Glade.

"Take a look at this instrument, Tang," he said. "That's a vibraphone." Tang listened to the vibraphone playing. He watched the sticks boing up and down.

He thought it was a wonderful, jazzy sound.

"It's making me feel so happy!" said Tang.

"Now I know what sort of song I'm going to write!" Tang started singing, "It's a hap-hap-happy day!" Then he thought, "I must go and sing it to the others!"

So, Tang jumped on a vine and swung off into the hot sunny jungle.

5

Tang found Drum by a tree.
"Hey Drum! Would you like
to hear my happy song?"

But Drum wasn't feeling
happy at all.

She couldn't reach a
yummy looking banana
at the top of the tree
and it was making her cross.

Tang decided to help Drum,
so he borrowed a piece of
driftwood from Todd.

He wafted the driftwood
at the banana until the
breeze made the banana
fall out of the tree.

Hooray!

But Drum was so
excited about her
banana, she
didn't want to hear
Tang's song.

Poor Tang!
"Perhaps I can play my
happy song to Zak," he thought.

But when Tang found Zak he
looked very annoyed.
"I can't make my bat and ball work!" said Zak.
"And I don't feel like hearing happy songs today!"

"Maybe I can help," said Tang. "Try thinking of a rhythm in your head. Then pat the ball to the same rhythm."

So Zak did just that. And it worked!

"Thanks, Tang!" Zak laughed as he bounced his ball.

But Zak was so busy playing that he didn't want to hear Tang's happy song.

9

"Perhaps Panzee would like to hear my happy song." Tang set off to find her in the Coconut Hut, but she wasn't there.

Instead, he found DJ Loose and the Beach Byrds.

"Would you like to hear my happy song?" Tang asked.

But everyone was too busy or too sleepy.

It was very hot in the Coconut Hut and the Beach Byrds were offering DJ Loose fruit smoothies to drink. But all DJ wanted to do was have a little sleep.

"Perhaps I can help,"
thought Tang.

To keep them busy, Tang
asked the Beach Byrds to
make him a drink instead.

The Beach Byrds were
very pleased to do this
and dashed off.

"Thank you, Tang.
I can have a bit of
peace now," smiled DJ.

"Great!" thought Tang.
"I can play my happy
song to DJ."

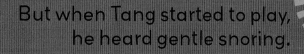

But when Tang started to play,
he heard gentle snoring.

DJ Loose had fallen asleep!
"I can't play DJ my song now,"
whispered Tang. "I might wake him up."

Nobody seemed to want to hear
his happy song.

Tang set off to find Panzee again.
As he was crossing the Beach,
he saw Gravel and Granite.

They looked very hot in the sunshine.
"Hi, Mr Gravel! Hi, Mr Granite!"
said Tang. "Would you like
to hear my happy song?"

"No," said Granite grumpily.

Gravel explained that Granite was
so hot it was making him very,
very grumpy.

And when Granite was grumpy
he couldn't count coconuts.
"Don't worry! I have an idea,"
said Tang and he dashed off.

A few moments later he returned
with a large white sheet.

"Here," said Tang. "That will keep the sun off!" Gravel was thrilled. "Thank you Tang," he said. "Now we can count coconuts all day!"

Tang wondered if this was a good moment to play his song.

"No," said Granite again. "We have to count coconuts now."

Poor Tang! Nobody wanted to hear his happy song.

He trudged off through the jungle. "Panzee will want to hear my song. She won't be feeling grumpy, cross, sleepy or hot. She's always happy."

But when Tang found Panzee in the Clubhouse she wasn't happy at all.

"I've lost the lovely red flowers I usually wear in my hair! It's making me really, really sad!" she cried.

Well, Tang didn't want Panzee to feel sad, so he helped her find the red flowers.

"Here they are!" he said. Panzee was thrilled. "Thank you! Thank you, Tang!" she said.

"Would you like to hear my happy song?" asked Tang.

"Oh – not now," replied Panzee. "I have to go and tell the others about my flowers." So she dashed off.

Tang had tried to play his happy song to everyone and nobody wanted to listen.

The only person he could find to play his song to was Yapple. This made Tang feel very sad. "I shouldn't be feeling sad," he said to himself.

"This is supposed to be a hap-hap-happy day."

So Tang tried to think of all the happy things that had happened that day.

He made Drum happy by getting her banana down. He made Zak happy by helping him bounce his ball.

He made DJ happy by letting him sleep.

He made Gravel and Granite happy by making hats for them.

And he made Panzee happy by finding her flowers.

"Making so many people happy makes me feel happy," smiled Tang.

He started to sing his happy song and very soon all the other ZingZillas joined in too.

They all wanted to say thank you to Tang for making them so happy today.

"Thank you, Tang!"

As they sang in the sunshine, the last coconut fell.
It was **Big Zing Time!**

And so, when the last coconut had fallen and the Moaning Stones had whizzed round the island, DJ Loose said, "It's that time of the day when we like to say: It's Big Zing Time! So take it away!"

And the ZingZillas played **Tang's Happy Song.** Even DJ Loose stayed awake long enough to listen. Afterwards, everyone agreed:

That was the best Big Zing EVER!